Dear Parent:
Your child's love of reading starts here!

Every child learns to read in a different way and at his or her own speed. Some go back and forth between reading levels and read favorite books again and again. Others read through each level in order. You can help your young reader improve and become more confident by encouraging his or her own interests and abilities. From books your child reads with you to the first books he or she reads alone, there are I Can Read Books for every stage of reading:

SHARED READING
Basic language, word repetition, and whimsical illustrations, ideal for sharing with your emergent reader

BEGINNING READING
Short sentences, familiar words, and simple concepts for children eager to read on their own

READING WITH HELP
Engaging stories, longer sentences, and language play for developing readers

READING ALONE
Complex plots, challenging vocabulary, and high-interest topics for the independent reader

ADVANCED READING
Short paragraphs, chapters, and exciting themes for the perfect bridge to chapter books

I Can Read Books have introduced children to the joy of reading since 1957. Featuring award-winning authors and illustrators and a fabulous cast of beloved characters, I Can Read Books set the standard for beginning readers.

A lifetime of discovery begins with the magical words "I Can Read!"

Visit www.icanread.com for information
on enriching your child's reading experience.

Pinkalicious®

The Royal Tea Party

For Mae

—V.K.

The author gratefully acknowledges the artistic and
editorial contributions of Daniel Griffo and Catherine Hapka.

I Can Read Book® is a trademark of HarperCollins Publishers.

Pinkalicious: The Royal Tea Party
Copyright © 2014 by Victoria Kann

PINKALICIOUS and all related logos and characters are trademarks of Victoria Kann. Used with permission.

Based on the HarperCollins book *Pinkalicious* written by
Victoria Kann and Elizabeth Kann, illustrated by Victoria Kann
All rights reserved. Manufactured in China.
No part of this book may be used or reproduced in any manner whatsoever without
written permission except in the case of brief quotations embodied in critical articles and reviews.
For information address HarperCollins Children's Books, a division of HarperCollins Publishers,
10 East 53rd Street, New York, NY 10022.
www.icanread.com

Library of Congress catalog card number: 2013950291

ISBN 978-0-06-218793-2 (trade bdg.)—ISBN 978-0-06-218791-8 (pbk.)

14 15 16 17 SCP 10 9 8 7 6 5 4 3 2 1
❖
First Edition

Pinkalicious®
The Royal Tea Party

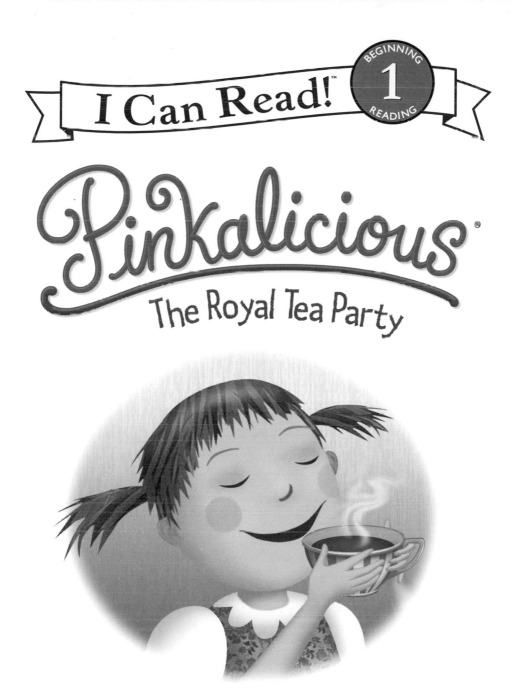

by Victoria Kann

HARPER

An Imprint of HarperCollinsPublishers

Goldilicious is the best

unicorn ever!

I want everyone to know it.

"You should throw her a party,"

Peter said.

That gave me a great idea.

"Listen, Goldie," I said.

(Goldie is her nickname.)

"I'm going to crown you

Princess Goldilicious."

There was a LOT to do
to get ready
for the
coronation.

"Can I do something?" Peter asked.

"Sorry, Peter," I said.

"This party is only for members
of the royal court."

I thought about what
Peter does the best.

Peter likes to eat.

"Maybe you could be

the royal taster," I said.

"That means you taste all the food

to make sure it's perfect."

"Great idea," Peter said.

"I can't wait to start!"

I decorated the backyard
with Goldie's favorite color:
PINK!

Then I went inside

and planned the perfect menu.

"What do you think, Peter?" I asked.

Peter had a little sip of tea.

"This tastes okay," Peter said.

"It's a little boring, though."

"Don't be silly," I told him.

"It's perfect!"

15

Soon my guests arrived.

"Come in, come in!" I cried.

"You're just in time to help

get Goldie ready."

"Can I help?" Peter asked.

"No, thanks," I said.

"But you can go to the kitchen
and take the food outside."

Peter went into the kitchen.

He was in there for a long time.

"What are you doing in there?"

I called.

"The royal taster is only supposed

to have *one* taste!"

"I'm just making sure
the food is perfect,"
Peter replied.
"I'm coming outside now."

Finally, Goldie was ready.

"Let the royal tea party begin!"

I declared.

My friends and I sat down.

Goldie had the place of honor.
I noticed that the food
looked a little different.

I sipped my tea.

"Pardon me a moment,"

I said to my guests.

Then I dragged Peter away.

"What did you do to the tea?"

I whispered.

"I made it better," Peter said.

"I used all my favorite foods.

I put maple syrup in one teacup.

I added peanut butter to another."

"I stirred strawberry jam
and vanilla yogurt
into the other teacups,"
Peter continued.

"As the royal taster, I felt
the sandwiches were tasteless,
so I made better ones
with ice cream instead of mayonnaise
and Goldfish crackers
instead of tuna fish."

"This is a disaster!" I cried.

I went back to apologize

to my guests.

"Yum!" Molly exclaimed.

"This sandwich is delicious!"

"My tea tastes yummy, too,"

Lila added.

"What's your secret, Pinkalicious?"

I tasted my tea again.

It tasted like maple syrup—

Hmm, it *was* good!

My friends didn't seem to mind.

The food tasted extra special.

Maybe this party
wasn't a disaster after all.
Maybe it was . . .
a perfect royal tea party!

"Let the coronation begin!" I said.

Goldie pranced forward.

"Goldilicious, you are the smartest, most beautiful unicorn ever."

I touched my wand to Goldie's horn.
"I hereby royally declare you
Princess Goldilicious!" I said.
"Hooray!" my friends cheered.

I gave Peter a new hat.

Then I touched my wand to his head.

"And I declare YOU

Sir Peter the Chef!" I said.

"Hear, hear!" said Peter.

"Who wants more?"